HOME-FIELD FOOTBALL

BY JAKE MADDOX

TEXT BY
THOMAS KINGSLEY TROUPE

ILLUSTRATIONS BY
SEAN TIFFANY

STONE ARCH BOOKS
a capstone imprint

Jake Maddox books are published by Stone Arch Books
A Capstone Imprint
1710 Roe Crest Drive
North Mankato, Minnesota 56003
www.capstonepub.com

Library of Congress Cataloging-in-Publication Data
  Home-field football / by Jake Maddox; text by Thomas Kingsley Troupe ; illustrated by Sean Tiffany.
     p. cm. — (Jake Maddox sport story)
  Summary: When his mother's job forces them to move to a rural area, Mason joins the Clearwater Middle School football team and finds that it will be up to him to teach them how to win.
  ISBN 978-1-4342-4008-8 (library binding) — ISBN 978-1-4342-4206-8 (pbk.)
  1. Football stories. 2. Teamwork (Sports)—Juvenile fiction. 3. Middle schools—Juvenile fiction. [1. Football—Fiction. 2. Teamwork (Sports)—Fiction. 3. Middle schools—Fiction. 4. Schools—Fiction.] I. Troupe, Thomas Kingsley. II. Tiffany, Sean, ill. III. Title.
  PZ7.M25643Hkm 2012
  813.6--dc23   2011052563

Graphic Designer: Russell Griesmer
Production Specialist: Danielle Ceminsky

Photo Credits: Shutterstock 43565725 (Cover & p. 64, 70, 71, 72), Shutterstock/Nicemonkey 71713762 (p. 3), Shutterstock/Justin S. 59461957 (Cover & p. 2, 3, 66, 67)

Printed in China.
032012   006677RRDF12

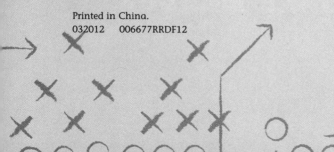

TABLE OF CONTENTS

CHAPTER 1
WELCOME TO NOWHERESVILLE

"It's not all bad, is it, Mason?" Mom asked as they stood in front of the moving van. It was parked on the driveway, up close to their new house.

"I'm not sure yet," Mason admitted. He wanted to say *It's worse than bad. This was the biggest mistake ever!* But he knew it wouldn't make a difference. His mom's job had taken the two of them to Clearwater Bluff.

It was a small town out in the middle of nowhere. And they were stuck there now.

Mason had never even seen the house before that day. Mom's work had found them a place to live, it was finalized within a day, and then they were packing.

"I know this isn't easy for you," Mom said. She set a box labeled KITCHEN down on the ground and stood next to her son.

They looked out at the fields across the street together. As if on cue, a tractor rumbled along the road and the farmer driving it waved to them.

"Oh, boy," Mason said, sighing.

He waved back to the farmer and managed a smile. He'd never seen anything like that back in the city.

He was used to living in a place where the only things on the roads were cars and neighbors' houses were just a few feet away. Clearwater Bluff was . . . different.

"It might take some getting used to," Mom said. She laughed. "Take a deep breath! When was the last time you breathed fresh air?"

Mason inhaled. The air smelled like manure from a nearby farm, but he kept that to himself.

"It's pretty great," Mason replied.

He wondered what his buddy Drew and the rest of his old football team would think of his new life. Just two weeks ago, Mason was still practicing with them, preparing for the season. Now, he was starting at a new school, hundreds of miles away from his friends and teammates.

There hadn't even been much time to say goodbye to all of his friends. Telling Coach Wells that he needed to leave the team was especially tough. He'd turned in his gear, shook hands, and that was it.

But that was ancient history now. Wishing he was back home wouldn't do any good.

"Let's get the rest of this unpacked," Mason suggested. He was eager to just get it over with.

"Sounds good," replied Mom.

Mason hopped up onto the truck and pulled a few boxes down. Mom wasn't used to driving anything bigger than her own car. The boxes had shifted a little during the trip. Luckily, everything looked like it had survived.

Making lots of trips back and forth, they lugged the boxes into the house. Mason was thankful that he and his mom didn't have a lot of stuff. But he wished they knew someone in town who could help them move the big things. He wasn't sure how they would manage the couch and dressers on their own.

Finally, they took a break and had ice-cold glasses of lemonade on the old front porch.

"Do you think you'll survive here?" Mom asked.

"I think so," Mason said. And when his mom hugged him, he knew he had to try. No matter what.

CHAPTER 2
TWENTY-TWO

As he walked down the hallway of Clearwater Middle School, the first thing Mason thought was, *This place is old.*

Back home, the lockers were newer, taller, and quite a bit wider. The maintenance staff even put fresh paint on them every year.

This school was different. When Mason found his locker, he noticed the lock was cracked and didn't turn easily.

"Great," Mason mumbled.

After trying three times and nearly shredding his hand, he finally got his locker open. He tossed his bag and lunch inside.

"You must be the new guy," said a boy a few lockers away. He was taller, with short cropped hair. "Mason, right?"

"Yeah," Mason said, looking around. "How did you know?"

"Dude," the kid said. "We've got twenty-one seventh graders this year. You make twenty-two. Everyone knows when a new kid starts."

Mason nodded. *Twenty-two kids? That isn't even the size of the football team back home,* he thought.

"I'm Kirk," the kid said. "You're a pretty big guy. Ever think about playing football?"

Mason smiled. "Funny you should ask," he said. "I need to see if it's too late to join the team."

Kirk shrugged and shut his locker. Something inside rattled and crashed to the bottom. "Probably not," he said. "It's not much of a team anyway. Just a bunch of guys with nothing better to do."

Mason couldn't believe what he was hearing.

"Talk to Coach Willman," Kirk suggested. "You'll see him in a few minutes."

Mason shook his head. "I've got history first period," he said. "I'll probably see him after school."

"Trust me," Kirk said. Together, they headed off down the nearly empty hall to class.

The bell rang as Mason found a seat. There were only nine other students in the classroom. Mason wondered if he'd ever get used to Clearwater Middle School.

The history teacher was a skinny, nervous-looking man. He wore glasses that looked two sizes too big for his face. The lenses were thick. His brown sweater vest had papers and pens sticking out of its pocket, and he wore a crooked polka-dotted bow tie.

When the teacher stood up and wrote MR. WILLMAN on the black board, Mason understood what Kirk had meant.

"He's the coach?" Mason whispered to Kirk.

Kirk nodded. "Yeah," he whispered. "That's Coach Willman."

CHAPTER 3
COACH WILLMAN

"Hello, Mason," Mr. Willman said as Mason walked up after class. "How's your first day of school going?"

"So far, so good," Mason replied. "I did have a question, though."

"And I've got an answer," Mr. Willman replied. "Might not be the right one, but I'll give it to you anyway." He laughed at his own joke a little too loudly.

"Funny," Mason said. "Um, about the football team. Kirk says you're the coach."

"The rumors are true," Mr. Willman replied with a nod. He pushed his glasses back up onto his nose. "Why? Did you want the job?"

"Um, no," Mason replied. *Was that another joke?* he thought. "I just wondered if I could join the team."

"Yes, yes, of course," Mr. Willman replied. "Practice starts today at 3:30 p.m."

"Oh," Mason said. "I don't even need to —"

"Welcome to the Clearwater Crocs Football team!" Mr. Willman said. "We'll pick positions at practice."

Mason was speechless. No tryouts? The players picked their positions?

17

What kind of crazy school is this? Mason wondered.

"Cool, thanks," Mason replied. "How did the Crocs do last year?"

Mr. Willman cleared his throat and shook his head. "You know, Mason," he said slowly, "I'm not sure. Mr. Haskins left last year, and they gave me the job. No one else wanted to be coach. If the Crocs were going to have a football team, I had to do it."

"Really," Mason said.

"I'm not much of a football fan," Mr. Willman finally admitted. He pulled a pen out and made a mark in a small notebook. "But I figure we'll put something together, right? How hard can it be?"

"Sounds good," Mason mumbled. "I'll see you after school, then."

"Looking forward to it!" Mr. Willman called as Mason left the room.

Kirk was waiting for Mason outside the classroom. "We're pretty much doomed, aren't we?" Kirk asked.

"It seems like it," Mason said, nodding. "Everything about the football program here is . . ."

"You don't need to say it," Kirk said. "But that's how things happen here. The coaches don't stick around long enough to build a good team. Every few seasons, a new guy gets to start over. Now it's poor Mr. Willman's turn."

As he and Kirk walked down the hall to class, Mason wondered, *Would Mom let me move back home to live with Drew, just for football season?*

CHAPTER 4
OLD GEAR

Mason called his mom's cell phone number from the school office. The school's phone was an old rotary phone that he couldn't figure out at first. A school secretary showed him how to spin the dial to enter the numbers. After a few tries, Mason got it to work.

"Hi," Mason said when his mom answered. "I'll be late coming home from school today."

"Did you get in trouble?" Mom asked. Before Mason could answer, she said, "I'm kidding! But . . . did you?"

"No," Mason replied. "I got on the football team and practice starts right after."

"Oh, your tryout must have gone well," Mom said.

"Sort of . . ." Mason said. "Mom, everything here is really different."

"I know, Mason," Mom said, "but you're playing football again. You'll feel at home soon. Thanks for giving this a chance."

"Sure, Mom," Mason said. "See you soon."

* * *

When Mason found the locker room, Kirk was there with a group of other guys. They all stood around in old shorts and T-shirts that looked like they hadn't been washed since last season.

"Here's the new guy," Kirk said. "This is Mason."

"As in jar?" a big guy asked. He elbowed a few of the others standing around him. "Get it? Like a mason jar?"

Kirk sighed. "Ignore Jerry," he said. "He thinks he's funny."

"I *am* funny," Jerry said, then smiled. He held out his gigantic, meaty hand. "Welcome to the team, Mason."

Mason shook hands with everyone on the team. They seemed like good guys. But no one seemed too concerned about practice.

Mason wondered if any of them even cared what position they would play.

They walked out to the practice field. Mason nearly twisted his ankle on the bumpy ground.

"Careful," warned Davis. "There's all kinds of holes out here."

And we're supposed to practice on this? thought Mason. He was used to a smooth, even field.

"Hey, fellas!" Coach Willman called. He stood in the end zone, waving to them. "Over here."

Scattered all around his feet were shoulder pads, helmets, and a couple of flat-looking footballs. Various pads for the football pants were spread out on the ground.

"This is practice gear, right?" Mason whispered to Kirk.

"Funny," Kirk muttered. "This is it."

"All right, guys," Coach Willman shouted. "I guess we'll just put on some gear and throw the ball around. Then we'll pick positions so we're ready for the game on Friday."

Friday?! Mason thought. *The first game is Friday? There's no way we'll be ready.*

Mason was starting to think he should forget the whole idea of playing football at his new school. Things were just too different here.

The rest of the guys picked through the gear. "I need the biggest helmet," Jerry called out. "Seriously, guys. Leave the biggest bucket for me."

"Giant head," Kirk whispered to Mason, who watched in amazement. Jerry's head really *was* big. "Every year it's the same thing. He can't find a helmet that fits."

Though the gear was old, it was still in decent shape. After a few minutes, Mason found a good set of shoulder pads, some shin and forearm guards, and a helmet. It had a loose face mask, but it fit.

Mason looked around at the other guys. Riley had his shoulder pads on backward. Bill was still struggling to slip his hip pad into the pocket of his girdle. And Davis was wearing flip-flops.

"Let's practice, Crocs!" Coach Willman shouted.

CHAPTER 5
PRACTICE MAKES PERFECT?

"What should we do, Coach?" a guy named Robert asked.

Coach Willman looked at the guys and shrugged. It was painful to watch the poor history teacher look around helplessly. Mason could see he was going to have to take charge.

"Why don't we just toss the ball around a bit?" Mason suggested.

Mason had the guys on the team line up across from each other. "Try this," he said. "We'll throw in a pattern."

He showed the team how the first guy would throw to the person across from him. That guy would catch it, turn, and throw it diagonally to the next person in line. It kept them constantly throwing and catching.

"Great idea, Mason," Coach Willman said, nodding. "This should keep us busy for the entire hour."

"Hour?" Mason asked in surprise. "Back at my old school, we practiced at least two hours every night. With the shape we're in, we could use the extra practice, Coach."

"An hour is all my schedule allows," Coach said. He shrugged. "I've got lessons to prepare, quizzes to write."

Mason sighed. "Okay," he said. "Then we could watch to see who's throwing straight and who catches more than half of the passes. Would that be all right, Coach?"

Coach Willman nodded.

"If someone drops the ball a lot or throws bad passes, we should pull them off to the side," Mason said. "This should help us pick our linemen and who might be our quarterback and receivers."

Coach Willman kicked at a rock in the field. "Shouldn't the *players* choose what position they want to play?" he asked.

Mason shook his head. "No way," he replied. "Half the team will want to be quarterback, and no one will want to be on the line."

"If you say so," replied Coach.

The Crocs ran the passing drill. After a while, Coach Willman had pulled almost everyone from the lines. Just four guys were left.

"Johnny, Billy, Wyatt, and Kirk," Coach called. "One of you will be our quarterback."

All four of the guys looked like their bike had just been stolen.

"Seriously?" Kirk asked. "Count me out. I know I don't want the job."

The other guys in the group shook their heads, too. Mason couldn't believe it. No one wanted what other players usually considered the best position on the team.

What is wrong with this town? Mason wondered.

CHAPTER 6
WHO WILL BE QB?

"Hey, Mason," Kirk said. "Since you know so much about football, why don't you be quarterback?"

The other guys nodded. Mason saw Coach Willman look at his watch. His hour of coaching was almost up.

"I'm not much of a quarterback," Mason admitted. "Back on my old team, I was the center. My best friend, Drew, was quarterback."

Mason smiled, remembering how fun it had been. "I'd fire the ball to him and work with the linemen to keep him safe," he said. "I'd like to play center again."

"Yeah," Davis said. "I don't want that job either."

"Great," Mason said. "But we still need at least one quarterback."

The four potential QBs stood silent. Kirk looked at the ground.

"Guys, this is a really important position," Mason said.

"How about we draw straws? Shortest straw is quarterback," Wyatt suggested. "That's fair."

Wyatt snatched up a stick and broke it into four pieces, making one extra small. "Here," he said, handing the sticks to Mason.

Mason turned his back to the candidates and shuffled the sticks around in his fist. He made the tops look even with one another.

Each of the quarterback finalists stepped up. Kirk drew first, pulling the stubby stick from Mason's hand.

"No way!" Kirk cried. "This is terrible!"

Just to be sure, the other guys pulled their sticks. It was settled. Kirk had drawn the shortest stick.

"Don't worry," Mason said. "I can help you. I learned a few things from Drew."

"Can you stop the big dudes on the other team from crushing me?" Kirk asked.

"I can try," Mason said. He shrugged. "I wouldn't be much of a center if I didn't stop a defensive tackle, right?"

Kirk looked up at the sky and shook his head. "Why me?" he cried.

Suddenly, Mason realized why everyone was acting weird. They were all scared. "Are you scared of getting knocked around?" Mason asked. "Is that why no one wants to be quarterback?"

"Yeah," Kirk replied. He kicked a stone loose from the soil and watched it tumble and bounce away. "And I'm not so good at throwing to a moving target."

Mason clapped his new friend on his shoulder pads. "I can definitely help you with that," Mason said.

CHAPTER 7
TIRE SWING

The Crocs stayed for an hour and a half after Coach Willman left. Positions were decided and assigned. Everyone seemed okay with their spot on the team.

Everyone except Kirk.

After practice, Mason and Kirk rode home on their bikes.

"You know we're not going to win on Friday, right?" Kirk asked. "I mean, we all know how to play, just not very well."

"Who knows what will happen on Friday?" Mason said. "Let's just try not to get completely destroyed on the field."

"Sounds good," Kirk said. He nodded to the right. "This is my house."

Mason followed Kirk up the driveway of a small white house. Like all of the yards in Clearwater Bluff, Kirk's yard was huge. In the front yard, a tire swing hung from a big tree.

"If you're not in a hurry to go in, I know how we can improve your passing game," Mason said.

"Yeah," Kirk said. "I'm pretty sure anything would help, right?"

"I think so," Mason said. "We'll work on your accuracy first. I see the perfect target you can aim for."

"Let me find a ball," said Kirk.

"Okay," Mason said, once Kirk had found his football in the garage. "I'll swing the tire back and forth —"

"And you want me to hit it with the football?" Kirk interrupted.

"Even better," Mason replied. "I want you to throw the ball through it."

It wasn't easy to do. Kirk completely missed the mark the first thirty times. Every time, Mason tossed it back and told Kirk to keep trying.

Kirk threw again and again. When the ball finally hit the tire for the first time, Kirk cheered. "Yes!" he shouted. "Progress!"

"Nice," Mason said with a smile. "Now, put it through the hole!"

"Right," Kirk muttered. "No problem."

After a while, Kirk could hit the tire every two out of three throws. But he still couldn't throw the football through the tire.

"I think you're throwing a little late," Mason said. "Throw it earlier than usual. Fire your pass a split second sooner. Aim for the O."

"Aim for the O," Kirk said, nodding. "Got it."

Kirk threw four more passes. Then, on the fifth try, the football whistled through the tire, the ball spiraling perfectly. It never even touched the rubber.

"It's good!" Mason shouted. He put his arms up like referee signaling a successful field goal.

"Wow," Kirk said. He rolled his shoulder around to loosen it up. "This is the most football I've ever played."

"It's a great start," Mason said. "We still need to work on snapping the ball and reading the backfield."

"Tomorrow," Kirk said, looking out at the horizon. The sunset was casting an orange glow all across Clearwater Bluff. "I need to eat."

"Deal," Mason said. He bumped fists with Kirk and headed to his bike. "We'll make a quarterback out of you yet."

"Thanks, Coach," called Kirk, laughing as Mason took off pedaling home.

CHAPTER 8
PRACTICE UNTIL DARK

After school the next day, the Crocs were suited up and ready to go on their rough-and-tough practice field.

Coach Willman set up a few old plays he'd found in the old coach's desk. Mason worked with the offensive line, setting up how to properly keep the defensive team back. Kirk threw to his receivers in the backfield and pitched the ball to his running backs.

Before anyone realized it, Coach Willman's hour was up.

"I hate to do this, guys," Coach said. "But I've got to go. I have a ton of work to do for classes this week."

"That's okay," Mason said, nodding. "We're having extra practices at my house every day until Friday's game. Is it cool if we bring the gear there?"

Coach Willman nodded. "That would be fine," he replied.

"If you think you could work on that stuff for your classes while we're practicing, you could stop by," Kirk suggested.

A slow smile crossed their history teacher's face. "You know," he said, fixing his glasses, "I might just do that."

* * *

At Mason's house, the guys marked off a section of the old farm field to use as a practice space. While some of the guys worked on the routes for their plays, the linemen practiced tackling each other.

Meanwhile, Mason tossed the ball to Kirk. "Ready to work on snaps?" he asked.

Kirk shrugged. "I guess so," he said. "If you think it's important."

"It's probably the most important part," Mason said. "A missed snap is a fumble. The other team can snatch it up and run it into the end zone."

"Great," Kirk muttered. "Now I have that to worry about."

"You'll be fine," Mason promised. "I'm a pretty decent center. I made sure Drew never missed a snap."

Mason got into position. Then he told Kirk where to go.

"Stand behind me with your hands low. Make a C with your hands," Mason called. "You'll watch the line and make sure everyone is where they're supposed to be. Then you can call for the snap," he added.

After four tries, Kirk got the hang of it. Mason showed him how to grip the ball and take a few steps back.

"You can see if the play is working and who's open," Mason said. "Of course, don't go too far back. We'll lose some major yardage if you get sacked."

"Got it," Kirk said. Then both of the boys saw Coach Willman walking over to them. He was holding an armload of papers.

"Look who's here!" Jerry shouted. "How's it going, Coach?"

Coach Willman waved, almost losing his paperwork. "I felt guilty being at home while you guys are working," he said. "I'll try coaching *and* correcting a test or two."

"Sounds good," Mason said. "We're just about to run some plays."

From then until dark, the Crocs played football. They knocked each other into the dirt, ran passing plays, and moved the ball down the field. On Wednesday and Thursday, they did more of the same, spending time on defense and special teams.

After their last practice on Thursday night, all of the Crocs lay on the grass. Their football gear was filthy and soaked with sweat.

"We're going to be too tired to play tomorrow," Wyatt said. "I can barely move."

"We'll be fine," Mason said. "We'll get onto their fancy field tomorrow night, and you'll forget about being sore."

The rest of the team was quiet. Mason wondered if they were scared, excited, or both. No matter what, he knew, game time was in less than twenty-four hours.

CHAPTER 9
FIRST GAME

The first game was tough for the Crocs. Near the end of the third quarter, the Crocs offense huddled up. Mason looked at the rest of the guys. They were breathing hard and sweating. They looked ready to quit.

Still, Mason was surprised that the team was playing as well as it was. Though the Titans led 28 to 18, the Crocs had scored three times.

"Are we still in this game?" Mason asked. Every head around him nodded.

"The other team's not as tired as we are," said Kirk.

Mason nodded. It was true. The Titans had enough guys to make up a separate offense, defense, and special teams. The Crocs players all had to play the whole game.

"Maybe not," Mason said. "But they're wondering about us. They didn't expect this kind of a team from Clearwater Bluff."

"They've got us by ten points," Robert, the left guard, said. "We need to score twice and keep them from moving downfield."

"Then that's the plan. There's no reason we can't win this game," Kirk said. Mason was surprised. Though he never wanted to be quarterback, Kirk was beginning to sound like the team's leader.

"Let's do it," Mason growled.

The rest of the team put their hands in the middle and shouted, "One, two, three, BREAK!"

* * *

Mason knew that a game could be lost with just one missed snap. But after a game of perfect snaps, he never expected what happened next.

Mason dug into the Titans' well-groomed field with his cleats. As he put his hand over the ball, he sensed something was wrong.

"Hut!" Kirk shouted. But his voice trembled.

Mason snapped the ball like he'd done a million times before, but Kirk's hands weren't there. The ball fell and tumbled behind the quarterback.

As Mason dug in against the Titans' defense, he saw Kirk scramble. The defensive ends came around the Crocs' offensive line. Kirk scooped up the ball.

It's too late, Mason thought, keeping his guy back.

The ends closed in. Kirk threw the ball high and deep before he was crushed. A moment later, wild cheers erupted from the stands. Despite the big tackle, Kirk had completed the pass!

"Touchdown!" The announcer shouted. "Number 19, Wyatt Gillman!"

Once the play was over, Mason scrambled to his feet. The defensive ends walked away, leaving the twisted wreck of Kirk on the ground. For a moment, Mason thought his friend had been knocked out.

Until he heard Kirk laughing.

CHAPTER 10
MAKE AN O

"Are you hurt or just crazy?" Mason asked. He helped Kirk to his feet. The referee blew the whistle to signal the end of the third quarter.

"Both, I think," Kirk replied. He smashed his shoulder pads into Mason's. "I never knew being tackled could be so much fun!"

"How did you complete that pass?" Mason asked. "You had two big Titans closing in on you."

Kirk shrugged. "I saw Wyatt break away and I fired," he said. "Got lucky, I guess."

Mason clapped as they approached the huddle. "Well, it was awesome!" he said.

"Are we going for two points?" Jerry asked.

Kirk nodded. "Sure," he said. "Why not?"

* * *

The Crocs didn't land the extra points, but they held the Titans on defense. However, when the Crocs were on offense, the Titans held them back, too.

Nothing worked for the offense. The running plays were shut down almost immediately. The Crocs lost yardage with every attempt. The ball was turned over again and again. Before they knew it, the game was almost over. The score was 28 to 24, Titans.

Coach Willman called a time-out. "Bring it in, guys," Coach said as the Crocs ran to the sideline. He fidgeted with his glasses. "Nothing is working out there."

"It's like they've learned all of our tricks," Mason said.

He watched as the Titans defense began high-fiving each other. They acted like they'd already won the game.

Mason looked at the scoreboard. There was 1:02 left on the clock. The Crocs needed a touchdown to win, but were almost 20 yards away from a first down.

The game was all but lost.

"I'm just so tired," Robert said, moaning.

Then Mason had an idea.

* * *

The Crocs slouched back onto the field. Every single one of them acted as though they'd been beaten and were too tired to play anymore.

Mason watched the defensive line get into position. They sneered and shook their heads.

"Finally giving up?" number 43 asked.

"Whatever," Mason said, groaning. He crouched over the ball. As Kirk got behind him, Mason whispered to the quarterback, "Tire swing."

Kirk called for the snap, and the Titans never knew what hit them. One moment, the Crocs were slouchy, exhausted players who looked like they'd already given up. The next moment, they were on fire.

Mason sprang forward and kept the defensive tackle back. The rest of his line did the same. Nothing the Titans did could break the wall.

Mason turned to see Kirk circle to the left and look downfield.

"Look for the Os!" Mason shouted.

He glanced past number 43 and saw Wyatt, Johnny, and Davis. Johnny cut in, shaking his defender. Once he was free, he formed an O with his hands.

Kirk wound up and fired the ball downfield. It sailed over everyone's heads in a perfect spiral and rocketed toward Johnny's open arms.

As the ball arrived, Johnny closed the O. He caught the football neatly.

The Titans scrambled after the wide receiver, but it was too late. Johnny was off like a shot. He ran the ball the last 23 yards into the end zone.

The small crowd of Crocs fans went wild in the stands.

"I can't believe it!" Kirk yelled as Mason and the rest of his team ran over. "We just won!"

Mason smiled and happily smacked the top of Kirk's helmet. "Yeah, we did!" Mason shouted.

As the Clearwater Bluff Crocs laughed and whistled in victory, Mason looked at the scoreboard. *Home: 28, Visitor: 30.*

Clearwater Bluff isn't home yet, Mason thought. He smiled. *But it's starting to feel like it.*

ABOUT THE AUTHOR

Thomas Kingsley Troupe writes, makes movies, and works as a firefighter/EMT. He's written many books for kids, including *Legend of the Vampire* and *Mountain Bike Hero*, and has two boys of his own. He likes zombies, bacon, orange Popsicles, and reading stories to his kids. Thomas currently lives in Woodbury, Minnesota, with his super cool family.

ABOUT THE ILLUSTRATOR

When Sean Tiffany was growing up, he lived on a small island off the coast of Maine. Every day, from sixth grade until he graduated from high school, he had to take a boat to get to school. When Sean isn't working on his art, he works on a multimedia project called "OilCan Drive," which combines music and art. He has a pet cactus named Jim.

GLOSSARY

accuracy (AK-yer-uh-see)—freedom from error

backfield (BAK-feeld)—the football players who line up behind the line of scrimmage

end zone (END ZOHN)—the area beyond the goal line at each end of the football field where points are scored

field goal (FEELD GOHL)—a score of three points in football made by kicking the ball over the crossbar during ordinary play

fumble (FUHM-buhl)—a ball that has been dropped while in play

offensive line (uh-FEN-siv LINE)—the offensive players that line up on the line of scrimmage; their primary job is to block the defensive players

snap (SNAP)—to put a football in play by passing or handing it backward between the legs

DISCUSSION QUESTIONS

1. Mason is not honest with his mom about his feelings. Why not? Do you think he should tell her the truth about how he feels about his new school?

2. Is it harder for teams at small schools to be strong competitors? Why or why not?

3. Do you think Mr. Willman is a good coach? What makes a good coach?

WRITING PROMPTS

1. Pretend you're Mason. Write a journal entry about your impressions of your new school on your first day.

2. None of the Crocs wants to be quarterback, which is typically the most popular position on the team. Write a persuasive essay to convince others that playing quarterback is fun and exciting.

3. The Clearwater Crocs have old uniforms and equipment. Imagine you are a member of the team and you need to ask for new equipment. Write a letter to the school board explaining why you need these items.

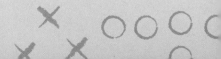

MORE ABOUT

Each football player on the field has a job to do. Here are some of the main positions.

ON THE OFFENSE

The **quarterback** is the leader of the offense. He moves the ball by throwing it to a receiver, passing it to a running back, or running with it himself.

The **running back's** main job is to run the ball toward the end zone.

The **wide receiver** is ready to catch passes from the quarterback.

Finally, the offensive line is made up of the **center**, two **offensive guards**, and two **offensive tackles**. During passing plays, the line protects the quarterback. During running plays, the line clears the way for the running back.

ON THE DEFENSE

The **defensive end's** job is to stop the running back during running plays, and to tackle the quarterback during passing plays.

The **defensive tackles** are often the largest and strongest players on the team. These players try to break up the offensive line and stop the running back on running plays.

Linebackers provide a second line of defense.

The **cornerback** usually guards the wide receiver, trying to keep him from catching passes. The safety helps the cornerback out in covering passes.

3 MORE GREAT BOOKS

JAKE MADDOX

BEHIND the Plate

JAKE MADDOX

STRIKER ASSIST

JAKE MADDOX

POINT GUARD PRANK

FROM
JAKE MADDOX

THE FUN DOESN'T STOP HERE!

DISCOVER MORE AT:

capstonekids.com

Authors and Illustrators
Videos and Contests
Games and Puzzles
Heroes and Villains

Find cool websites
and more books like this one
at www.facthound.com.

Just type in the Book ID:
9781434240088
and you're ready to go!